GANEKWANE AND THE GREEN DRAGON

FOUR STORIES FROM AFRICA

CORLIA FOURIE
ILLUSTRATED BY CHRISTIAN ARTHUR KINGUE EPANYA

ALBERT WHITMAN & COMPANY
MORTON GROVE, ILLINOIS

Library of Congress Cataloging-in-Publication Data

Fourie, Corlia.
Ganekwane and the green dragon: four stories from Africa / by Corlia Fourie;
illustrated by Christian Arthur Kingue Epanya.
p. cm.
Contents: Hlaulu and the beast in the forest — The middle sister and the tree —
The girl with the laughing voice — Ganekwane and the green dragon.
ISBN 0-8075-2744-0
1. Children's stories, Afrikaans—Translations into English. [1. Africa—Fiction. 2. Short stories.]
I. Epanya, Christian Arthur Kingue, ill. II. Title.
PZ7.F8254Gan   1994   93-45922
[Fic]—dc20   CIP
                                              AC

Text © 1992 by Corlia Fourie.
Illustrations © 1994 by Christian Arthur Kingue Epanya.
Design by Sandy Newell.
Text is set in Century Expanded.

English translation by Madeleine van Biljon.
First published simultaneously in Afrikaans and in English
in 1992 by Human & Rousseau (Pty) Ltd.
Cape Town, South Africa.

Published in 1994 by Albert Whitman & Company,
6340 Oakton Street, Morton Grove, Illinois 60053.
Published simultaneously in Canada by
General Publishing, Limited, Toronto.
Printed in the United States of America.
10 9 8 7 6 5 4 3 2 1

*T*o my mother, who was never too tired to read fairy
tales to me, and to Judith (Tombani) Mbokaze, who is always willing
to teach me about the Zulu culture.

C.F.

*T*o Françoise and Marthe, my beloved daughters.

C.A.K.E.

The tales in *Ganekwane and the Green Dragon*
are made-up stories with their origins in the
African oral tradition as well as the traditional
fairy tale of Western Europe. What I personally
like about these two traditions, and have employed
in *Ganekwane*, is the fact that the "underdog"
wins against all odds. But as a woman, it was
also important for me to create more active
heroines than the mainly passive ones I came to
know from both of these storytelling traditions.
All the stories were originally written in
Afrikaans. The names of the characters have
their origins in the Zulu language.

—*Corlia Fourie*

GLOSSARY

assegai (A si ghy) - a slender, iron-tipped spear of hard wood, used especially by southern African tribesmen.

baobab (BAYOH bab) - an African tree having an enormously thick trunk and large, edible pulpy fruit that hangs down on stalks.

duiker (DAY kir) - a small African antelope, widespread in southern African savannah and bush.

kaross (ki RAHS or ka RAHS) - a cloak or sleeveless jacket like a blanket made of hairy animal skins, worn by the indigenous peoples of southern Africa. Also, a rug of sewn skins used on a bed or on the floor.

kei-apple (KY ap puhl) - densely spiny shrub used for hedges, abundant in the Transkei area of South Africa. Its fragrant but acidic fruit is used for jam and jelly.

marsh fig - a tree found in coastal swamp forests in Zululand. The figs are big and bright red when ripe.

marula tree - the common name for *Sclerocarya birrea*, a tree common in the hotter parts of South Africa. It has a dense foliage, and its fruit is used for jam and jelly and for making beer.

mealies - maize, millet, a corncob.

putu porridge (POO too) - traditional African preparation of maize flour, cooked to the consistency of stiff porridge, sometimes to dry crumbs, eaten with a thick, naturally soured milk, or with meat and gravy.

sand apple - a creeping shrub, common in sandy places, with a fragrant fruit tasting somewhat like an apple.

sangoma (sahn GAW ma) - in southern Africa, a witch doctor, usually a woman, claiming supernatural powers of divination and healing.

sickle bush - a small tree or bush of the bushveld with feathery leaves, flowers with two-colored mauve and yellow spikes, and long, narrow pods. Chewed leaves are used as a quick first-aid remedy for different afflictions such as insect bites, sore eyes, and toothaches.

springbuck (or springbok) - a common southern African gazelle, characterized by the habit of leaping when excited or disturbed.

stinkwood tree - a southern African tree belonging to the laurel family. The wood is quite hard and usually has a dark color. It is in great demand for furniture. (When the stinkwood is cut, it gives off a disagreeable smell.)

tree fuchsia (FYOO shah) - a small tree, often with trailing branches, found everywhere from coastal areas to arid tableland to evergreen forests. The flowers are brick red and orange. The Zulus consider the tree a charm against evil, and twigs are burnt when offering sacrifices to ancestral spirits.

umuthi (u MOO tee) - African medicines, spells, and herbs, etc. used in therapeutic treatment, or in witchcraft or magic. (The word *muti* is now commonly used in South African English.)

veld - open country, bearing bushes or shrubs, or thinly forested. Characteristic of parts of southern Africa.

warthog - a wild pig which has pronounced warts on its face and bristly grey skin. It is common on the African savannah.

yellowwood tree - any of several trees of the southern African *Podocarpus* family which have a yellow wood. Very valuable for furniture and carpentry.

PRONUNCIATION OF CHARACTERS' NAMES

Ganekwane (gah nee KWA nee)
Hlaulu (SHLAH lu)
Kwobu Khuni (KWO bu KOO nee)
Ukuhleka (u ku SHLEH kah)

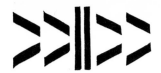

HLAULU AND THE BEAST IN THE FOREST

Once upon a time there was a girl called Hlaulu of the red beads because she liked wearing red beads around her neck, her waist, and her ankles.

Every morning Hlaulu's mother gave her a pot of putu porridge to take to a sick old woman who lived on the other side of the forest.

Hlaulu's mother only told her once to take the long way around because she knew Hlaulu wouldn't dare walk through the forest. For many moons, no one in the little village had walked through the forest. Not the big, strong men and women, and certainly not the children. For everyone in the village knew that a terrible beast named Kwobu Khuni lived there. Though no one had ever seen Kwobu Khuni, everyone could hear him. He screamed during the day, and at night he screamed even more. His shrieking was so frightful that the lions in the veld began roaring, and the village dogs howled.

The people would say, "Kwobu Khuni is very angry tonight. Beware of Kwobu Khuni."

Then the men and women stayed in their huts, sitting close to one another and holding the children in their laps.

And everyone was quiet. Everyone waited. No one knew whether one day Kwobu Khuni might storm out of the forest and attack the village.

During the day it wasn't so bad. One would be able to see Kwobu Khuni coming, should he decide to attack. One would be able to do something—maybe hide under a bush or climb a tree. Or all the men could grab their assegais and attack him together.

So because she was scared of Kwobu Khuni, Hlaulu walked all the way around the forest with the little pot of putu porridge on her head.

It was a long way to walk. A long way with the sun on her back as she went, a long way with the sun in her eyes as she returned. And with each step she took, the full pot felt heavier and heavier until Hlaulu thought there must be a stone in it. On the way back it wasn't the pot that bothered her, it was the endless walk.

But the old woman was very pleased to get the putu porridge—so pleased that every day she told Hlaulu a story, but only after eating a few mouthfuls of putu porridge.

One day the old woman told Hlaulu the story of the girl and the beast in the forest. "Once upon a time there was a girl who always had to walk around the forest because a beast lived in the forest. One day the girl got tired of having to take such a roundabout path. She was also curious to see what the beast of the forest looked like.

"So the girl slipped into the forest, as silently as a small duiker, and waited until she saw the beast coming."

"What did he look like?" Hlaulu asked, wide-eyed.

"Ugly, very ugly. He was almost as big as an elephant and had the fur of a hyena and the face and paws of a baboon. And his tail stuck straight up in the air like a warthog's."

"What happened then?" Hlaulu asked in a thin little voice, as

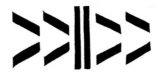

though she'd just heard the beast screaming outside the hut. "What did the beast do to the girl?"

The old woman made Hlaulu wait for a moment, and then she said, "Nothing. The beast didn't do anything to her because he didn't see her. She hid silently in the bushes and watched him.

"She saw the beast tear a buck to pieces and gobble up the whole thing, horns and all. She also saw that the beast liked wild figs and other sweet fruits, and she had a clever idea."

"What kind of clever idea?" Hlaulu asked.

"She slipped out of the forest as softly as she had slipped in," said the old woman.

"The following morning she took a pot of putu porridge and honey into the forest. She moved very softly, but the beast heard her and waited for her.

"She had barely entered the forest when he grabbed her! He wanted to gobble her up right away. But she freed one of her hands and tossed a clump of putu porridge and honey into the beast's mouth, and when he tasted it he drooled with delight.

"The girl ran back to the village, and as she went she dropped bits of putu porridge and honey. The beast followed the trail right out of the forest. And in the open veld, the girl's brothers stabbed him to death. That was the very last time anyone was afraid to walk through the forest."

Hlaulu thought about the story. Then she put the empty pot on her head, said goodbye to the old woman, and went on her way.

As she walked, Hlaulu talked to herself. "I can do what the girl did

and throw Kwobu Khuni honey and putu porridge." But then she changed her mind. "No, that was only a story. Who knows whether Kwobu Khuni likes honey and putu porridge?" She walked a little farther, then said to herself, "I can also move silently as a small duiker, and I can also hide in the forest and watch the beast."

She decided to do just that.

Softly, softly, she slipped into the forest. She didn't step on twigs, she didn't brush against branches, and she barely breathed.

Then she heard something groaning. She crept under a bush and peered out. She saw it was the beast of the forest. It was Kwobu Khuni. And she saw that he looked like the beast in the story. He even had the upright tail of a warthog.

But Kwobu Khuni wasn't eating meat and fruit like the beast in the story. No, Kwobu Khuni ran around in circles. He groaned. Then he suddenly dug up the roots of a plant. He chewed on them and groaned even more loudly, and more loudly. He groaned so loudly that the noise struck Hlaulu like thunder, like all the voices in a village screaming together, like the trumpeting of many elephants.

Then Kwobu Khuni rushed to a tree. He put his paw to his ugly face and screamed, "Hau! Hau!" Then he stuck his head into a hole in the ground and screamed into it.

Hlaulu no longer wondered about Kwobu Khuni. She no longer wondered why he screamed during the day and especially at night. She knew. She, too, had crawled about one night, screaming and clutching her cheek. And she knew what to do.

She ran out of the forest—ran to the small sickle bush which grew

near her hut. She lifted the little pot off her head and filled it with leaves from the sickle bush. Then she replaced the pot on her head and hurried back to the forest.

At the sickle bush and on the way to the forest, she could hear Kwobu Khuni screaming. But she was no longer scared of his loud cries.

Kwobu Khuni was screaming so loudly and wildly with pain that Hlaulu reached him before he saw her. And then he had such a fright that he fell over backwards into the bushes and just lay there, his huge eyes wide and his huge mouth open.

Quickly Hlaulu popped a leaf from the sickle bush into his mouth, and then another, and another. Then she pushed handfuls of leaves into his wide, open mouth. "Chew," she said.

And the beast of the forest, huge old Kwobu Khuni, ugly old Kwobu Khuni, old sore-tooth Kwobu Khuni, sat up and chewed the leaves. He chewed until there was spit and leaves all over the place. He chewed and he chewed.

After a while, he stopped chewing. He did not scream or howl. He just looked curiously at Hlaulu. Slowly, he put out his large paw and touched the beads around Hlaulu's neck, and he touched the beads around Hlaulu's waist, and he touched the beads around Hlaulu's ankle. He made small whimpering noises almost like a baby makes when it wants something from its mother.

"He wants my beads," Hlaulu thought, "but I'm not going to give them to him." Then she thought, "He's quite a sweet old monster. Maybe I'll give him one string of beads. Just one." Hlaulu unfastened

the string around her ankle and handed it to Kwobu Khuni.

Kwobu Khuni jumped for joy, making the forest boom and frightening the birds out of the trees. He danced in circles and kissed the beads. He danced so hard, the grasshoppers fled. Then of course, he wanted more beads.

But Hlaulu had already put her empty little pot on her head and walked out of the forest.

Now the forest was quiet. It was so quiet that the people of the little village could hear the birds chirping, so quiet that they could hear the cicadas singing, so quiet that they could hear Kwobu Khuni walking.

But sometimes when the moon was a pot-bellied curve in the sky, or when it was very cold, they would hear again that terrible screaming.

When it sounded as though the whole forest shivered with pain, Hlaulu, no matter whether it was day or night, walked into the forest with her clay pot on her head. There she found old sore-tooth Kwobu Khuni, and she stuffed into his mouth the leaves of the sickle bush.

And now Hlaulu took the short cut through the forest. When Kwobu Khuni saw her, he picked fruit for her from the highest branches of the trees.

And Hlaulu took this fruit to the old woman who lived on the other side of the forest.

THE MIDDLE SISTER
AND THE TREE

Once upon a time three sisters lived in a hut in the middle of a great grassy plain.

When they shared food or anything else, the eldest and the youngest sisters always knew what they wanted, but the middle sister thought for a long time before making a choice. It took her so long that the other two were already lying on the sleeping mat or had eaten some of the wild figs when she said what she wanted. So long did it take her to decide that her sisters never asked her which game she wanted to play. They simply told her.

But the sisters didn't spend the whole day playing. They also worked. Every day they walked down to the river to fetch water for their mealies.

One morning on the way to the river, the sisters saw a grey wildcat stalking a small bird that was searching for seeds.

Just when the wildcat was about to pounce, the three sisters ran and—shoo! shoo!—chased him away.

"Thank you very much," said the little bird, who had only seen the grey wildcat when the sisters had made it run away. "You may each have one wish, and whatever you wish for you'll get. But remember, only one wish each."

"A kaross," the eldest sister said immediately. "I can sleep on it at

night and wear it over my shoulders when it's cold."

"I want beads," said the youngest sister. "Beads for my head and my neck and my ears and my arms and my waist and my ankles. Lots and lots of beads!"

The middle sister said nothing. She simply stood there thinking and thinking and thinking.

"What about you?" the little bird asked after a while. "What would you like?"

"It's very difficult," said the middle sister. "Only one wish, and there are so many things I could wish for. I simply don't know yet." Her sisters laughed because they didn't believe the middle sister would ever be able to decide.

But the little bird said, "Think long and hard. I'll be back tomorrow; then you can tell me." And saying so, he flew away.

Early the next morning when the sisters woke up, they saw a kaross and a great many beads in front of the hut.

The eldest and the youngest sisters were very pleased.

"How stupid you were," said the eldest sister, "not to choose immediately."

"Yes," said the youngest. She fastened a string of beads around an ankle.

"How do you know the little bird will return?"

"He'll come back," said the middle sister. And after she had watered the mealies, she went to sit on a rock to think.

Perhaps she should ask for a new hut because the roof leaked when it rained. No, wait a moment, a larger patch of mealies would be

better; then they would be sure of enough food. Or maybe she could wish for the river to be nearer their home; then they wouldn't have to walk so far for water.

She thought for so long, the sun shifted to the middle of the sky and was burning the crown of her head. "Goodness, but it's hot," she thought. And then she knew what she wanted.

At that moment the little bird came flying up. "Do you know what to wish for by now?" it said.

"I wish there were a big tree near our hut. Then we could sit in its shade when it's hot," said the middle sister.

"That's a good wish," said the little bird, and it flew away.

The middle sister told her sisters about her wish. They all woke up very early the next morning and ran outside. But nothing was there.

The eldest sister said, "That was a really stupid wish. How on earth can a small bird fly here with a large tree in its beak?"

"He told us we could wish for anything," said the middle sister.

Chirp, chirp. They heard bird noises in the tall grass. And when they looked, truly, there was the little bird.

"I pushed the seed into the ground here. Just here." He showed the middle sister. "You must water the seed every day. Every day, remember. Then the seed will grow and become a small tree. And the small tree will grow and become a big, a very big tree, indeed."

"What a stupid wish." The youngest sister laughed as she played with her beads. "All your wish has given you is a lot of work."

"You made a good wish," the little bird told the middle sister. "If you do as I've told you, the tree will grow fast. Yes, after three full

moons, the tree will be large and strong. It's a marula tree. It will give you much more than shade."

Every day the middle sister fetched water for the seed, and after a few days there was a small tree, which was growing bigger very quickly. Sometimes the girl would stand next to the little tree simply to see it grow. Very soon the tree was so large that she could sit in its shade. And not long after that, the tree was so big that she could climb it. Now the middle sister no longer sat under the tree. No, she sat in the tree.

Her two sisters laughed at her. They laughed because again she was doing the difficult thing. "It's much easier to sit under a tree than in it," they said.

But the middle sister had found a comfortable seat from which she could see clearly through the branches, and nobody could see her from the ground.

One morning after she had finished her tasks, the middle sister climbed into the tree again. She watched the clouds drifting by and the birds flying by . . . and she fell asleep.

She was awakened by angry voices and screams and saw that warriors had captured her sisters! She saw them burning the hut and the mealie patch. She saw the leader hanging the kaross around his own shoulders, and the others sharing the beads among themselves.

When the warriors left with her sobbing sisters, the middle sister also burst into tears.

"Why are you crying?" the little bird asked. He was sitting on a branch just above her head.

"Because I made such a stupid wish," said the middle sister. "If I had waited, I could now wish for my sisters to be free."

"But you made a very good wish," said the little bird. "You have a tree. A marula."

"And of what use is the tree to me now? I have no food. I have no hut to live in. And my sisters are gone." She wept again.

"Look under the tree," said the little bird.

The middle sister looked and saw ripe yellow fruit lying under the

tree. She climbed down and ate until her stomach was full.

Then the little bird told her, "Fill a whole pot with fruit and take it to the people who captured your sisters."

The middle sister obeyed the bird. She put the full pot on her head and walked in the direction her sisters had been taken.

Three times she saw the sun jump into the sky, and three times she saw the plains swallowing the sun. Then she reached the village of the people who had captured her sisters.

When the warriors came to capture her as well, she said, "I have brought you a gift." And she took down the pot. She looked into the pot and saw that the fruit had fermented and become a drink.

The warriors tasted. Hmmm. They drank more and more, until they became very drunk and just lay there in the sun, the flies zooming about their heads.

The middle sister ran to the hut where her two sisters were tied with grass ropes. She freed them, and all three went back to the marula tree.

After that day all three sisters lived in the tree. And the tree gave them food. They took turns standing watch and could see the warriors coming a long way off. Then they sat quietly in the tree until the warriors went away again. In this way the tree looked after the sisters for the rest of their lives.

THE GIRL WITH THE LAUGHING VOICE

Once upon a time there was a clever chief with many sons but only one daughter, whom he loved very much.

When he started getting older, he said, "I'm looking for a clever man who will care for my beloved daughter, Ukuhleka, so that her voice will always sound like a babbling brook and singing birds and a light breeze in a forest."

Then he invited all the people to a great feast.

The women filled the cooking pots with buffalo meat and springbuck meat. They roasted guinea fowl, wild fowl, and partridges. And the baskets were filled with wild figs and the fruit of the marula trees, which the children had gathered. Delicious! Hmmm. And honeycombs! Of course there were honeycombs.

The drums would beat all through the night—*boom! boom! boom!*—and the people would dance until they fell down in a faint. But before all that, the chief announced that he wanted to speak.

He said, "The young man who brings me the king of the beasts, alive, and puts in my hand the seed of the most wonderful tree in the world, and whispers my secret name in my ear, shall have my daughter, Ukuhleka, as his wife."

After the night of the feast, many young men tried to win Ukuhleka of the laughing voice. Everyone liked her because she joked

and sang and danced as if she were always happy.

Some of the young men first went looking for the seed. They climbed mountains, searched in bushes and along rivers, in dry places and in places where it was wet and muddy.

Others first tried catching lions. They carried spears and shields and assegais. And they took the trails through bushes, across sandy wastes, and in ravines.

Others went to speak to sangomas, or went to caves to talk to spirits, or climbed mountains to wait for the answers to fly to them like birds to their nests.

Those who had first gone looking for the seed came back with seeds of the baobab, marsh fig, sand apple, tree fuchsia, sickle bush, yellowwood and stinkwood trees. Each time, the chief shook his head. They were good seeds from good trees, he agreed, but none of those trees seemed the most wonderful in the world.

Some of the men who had gone lion hunting came back with lion skins or lion cubs. No one came back with a big live lion. Some men didn't come back at all.

Many names were whispered into the chief's ear—names that had something to do with cleverness, or with the weather, or strong animals, or with power. But the chief only shook his head. No one knew the right name.

After three full moons the chief said to his daughter, "Ukuhleka, I'll have to think of easier tasks for the men to do. Otherwise, you'll never get a husband to look after you."

"Easier tasks?" Ukuhleka exclaimed, and laughed. "Wait a while,

Father, and see if *I* can't do these tasks."

Then the chief laughed and said, "My dear daughter is really very funny."

And he laughed until the tears streamed out of his eyes and he had a stitch in his side.

But the following morning he wasn't laughing any longer, because when the sun was hot on the crown of his head, he heard for the first time that Ukuhleka was gone. The other young girls told him that she had left very early that morning, carrying a basket.

The chief summoned his warriors. He wanted to send them to the four corners of the earth. There was to be no rest until they had found Ukuhleka.

But . . . who was laughing like that?

It was a girl. There was only one girl with such a laugh. And yes, it was Ukuhleka. She came walking across the veld, a big basket in her hand.

The chief smiled broadly and opened his arms in joy.

"What do you have in the basket, my daughter?" he called before she had even reached him.

When she stood in front of him, she replied, "The king of the beasts, dear Father."

How was this possible? Perhaps a newborn lion cub?

But no, it wasn't a lion. He could hear birdsong.

"Why do you say this is the king of the beasts, my daughter?" he asked when she showed him a small bird with a yellow throat and green feathers on its back.

"I wanted to go and catch a lion, Father, because like the men, I thought a lion was the king of the beasts. I watched the lion. Don't be afraid; he was fast asleep. Then a bee appeared and stung the lion, and the lion jumped up and roared and swatted and snapped, but he couldn't bite the bee. So I thought the tiny bee must be the king of the beasts. But just then this little bird flew past and swallowed the bee. So here, Father, I have brought you the king of the beasts."

The chief laughed, amazed and proud. "Did you hear?" he asked his people. "See how easily it was done. But Ukuhleka, my daughter, I won't allow you to wander off again. You may not go and search for the seed of the most wonderful tree in the world."

"There's no need to search," said Ukuhleka. "The most wonderful tree in the world grows in our village."

"Here? But we have only sweet thorn trees."

Ukuhleka picked a seed pod and put it in the chief's hand.

"The sweet thorn is the most wonderful tree in the entire world."

"Why do you say that, my daughter?"

"It gives us shade. The children are very fond of the gum, and the dry wood makes a good fire. And when the sweet thorn tree blooms, the yellow flowers attract bees, and the whole veld and the village smell of honey. Our cattle can feed on the flowers, the pods, and the seeds. And we use the bark to make thongs. We even use the sharp, white, straight thorns to pin our hides and other things together, and the children use them as horns for their clay cattle. The thorns are weapons, as well."

"Weapons? What do you mean, my daughter?"

"Do you remember when the buffalo chased you, Father? You dived under a sweet thorn tree, and the buffalo ran into the branches and thorns. He died there."

In amazement the chief exclaimed, "You're right, my daughter, the sweet thorn is surely the most wonderful tree in the world! Now all you have to do is to whisper my secret name in my ear."

The chief bent down, and Ukuhleka whispered in his ear, "Uku."

Surprised, he asked, "How do you know this? Do I talk in my sleep?"

"No," said Ukuhleka. "But, my dear Father, I didn't think you would let your only daughter's name be too far from your own."

The chief said proudly, "My beautiful daughter is also a clever daughter. She knows my secret name but has never said it aloud for my enemies to hear. And such a clever daughter can choose her own husband."

"Thank you, Father," Ukuhleka said. "But I don't want a husband—at least not yet. If I change my mind, you'll be the first person I tell."

"That is fine, my daughter," said the chief, "because I realize now that you are the best person to look after yourself."

GANEKWANE AND THE GREEN DRAGON

Once upon a time there was a group of people who built their village high up against a mountain so that they could see their enemies coming from afar— enemies such as the people from other tribes, and wild animals such as lions and leopards, elephants and rhinoceroses.

But one day a green dragon climbed over the mountain from the other side and went to live in a cave higher up than the village. The green dragon belched smoke and fire and frightened the people. So the chief sent a messenger with copper bangles to the green dragon.

The messenger said, "We know you aren't really cruel, dear dragon. We know you've got a kind heart hidden beneath your green scales. We know if we bow down low before you, you'll do us no harm, dear sweet old dragon."

The dragon looked at the man with the copper bangles, and he listened to him, as well. When he had finished looking and listening, he swallowed the man and the copper bangles.

The following day the chief sent another messenger to the dragon. This messenger brought the dragon a lion's skin. The messenger knelt in front of the dragon and said, "O mighty monster, O greatest of beasts, O dragon of dragons—"

And he was still carrying on in this manner when the dragon swallowed him and the lion's skin.

On the third day the chief sent another messenger to the dragon.
The messenger lay down before the dragon. Then he lifted his head
just a little — just enough so that the dragon could hear him speak.

"O prince of dragons, you are truly fierce. O king of dragons, we
cannot fight against you because we aren't dragons. We are only poor
little human beings."

"And that's why you taste so good!" the dragon roared, and
swallowed the third messenger.

The chief was at his wits' end. He asked the advice of the sangoma
of the tribe. Perhaps there was something the sangoma could do to
make the dragon disappear.

But the sangoma only shook his head. Then he said, "I can make
warts disappear and cure headaches. I can make a boy fall in love with
a girl. But I cannot make dragons disappear."

"Do something," the chief said angrily.

The sangoma threw his bag of bones on the ground and looked
carefully at the way they had fallen. At last he said, "The bones are
talking. The bones say the story grandmother must come here."

Immediately the chief sent someone to fetch the story
grandmother. And when she arrived, the sangoma said, "The bones
say the story grandmother must go to the green dragon. The story
grandmother must tell tales to the green dragon. Good tales. Many
tales. Then the green dragon will forget about us."

But the story grandmother laughed like a hen cackling. Her face
creased like a kei-apple which had lain in the sun for too long, and her
two yellow-white eyeteeth jutted out of her mouth.

She said, "I'm too old and too tired. The green dragon won't have the patience to listen to me. But my grandchild Ganekwane is young and lively, and she knows all my stories."

Then the chief and the sangoma and all the villagers said, "Yes, Ganekwane must go to the green dragon. She is the prettiest girl in our village. The green dragon won't gobble her up."

Her grandmother and all the other women helped Ganekwane to dress prettily. They gave her a dress of leopard skin, as well as ivory and copper bangles. And they plaited her hair in many small plaits.

Then her grandmother gave her a leaf of the stinkwood tree to put under her tongue. The leaf would help her tongue to find the right words. Now Ganekwane was ready to climb to the monster's cave.

The people of the village climbed with her until they heard the dragon huffing and puffing up in the cave. Then they swung around and ran down the mountain, past the village, and into the veld.

Only Ganekwane remained. Only Ganekwane climbed higher. Only Ganekwane climbed to the cave where the green dragon lived.

"Who are you?" asked the green dragon. "And why are you standing? Why don't you fall on your knees like everyone else?"

"I am Ganekwane."

"You are very pretty, Ganekwane. You'll probably taste delicious, as well." The green dragon stuck out his tongue and licked his lips.

Ganekwane was very frightened, but she tried not to show it. She said, "You'll be sorry if you swallow me."

"Why? Is there fire on your skin?"

"No."

"Do you have an assegai behind your back?"

"No."

"Are there stones between your toes?"

"No."

"And even if you had, I still wouldn't be scared of you. I swallow people, stones, assegais, and fire without feeling it. Why would I be sorry if I swallowed you?"

"Because I tell beautiful tales."

"What are tales?" the dragon asked.

Then Ganekwane told the green dragon about Hlaulu and the beast in the forest.

The dragon listened.

When Ganekwane had finished the tale, the dragon said, "Another tale, Ganekwane."

And as he said this, his skin burst like an insect's, and he crept out with a new skin. But he wasn't bigger as insects are when they shed their skins. He was smaller!

Then Ganekwane told him about the middle sister and the tree. She thought so hard about the right words that the stinkwood leaf jumped out from under her tongue, flew out of her mouth, and fell in front of the dragon's paw.

The story girl had such a fright that she swallowed her words. But the green dragon didn't notice. "What happened then?" he asked.

So Ganekwane continued her story. And the dragon listened, his green head tilted to one side. He listened and listened. And while he was listening, he put his paw on top of the leaf.

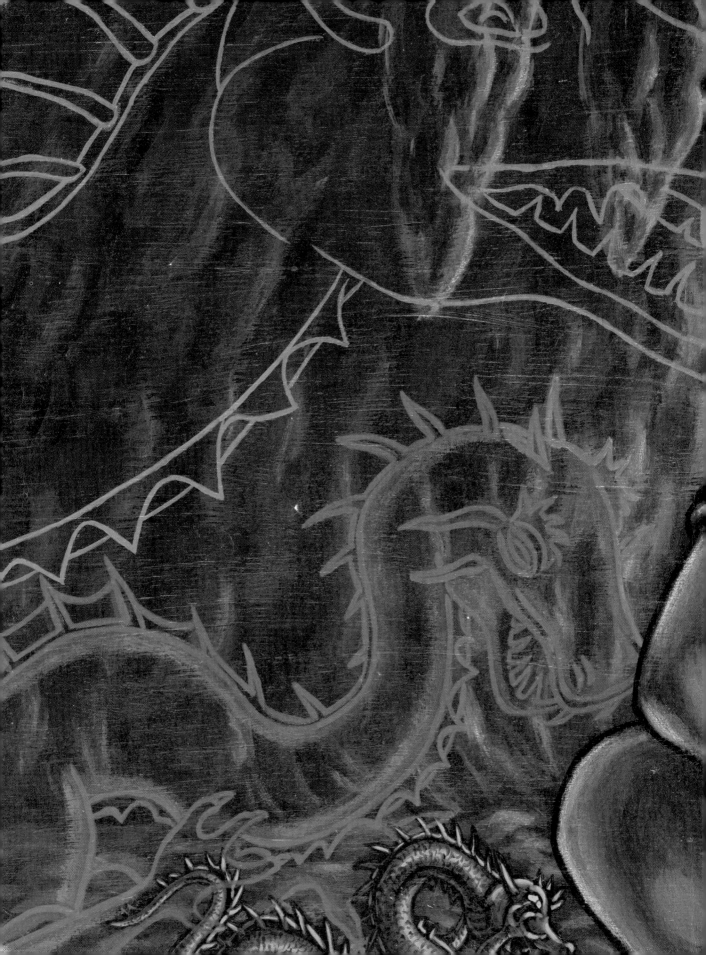

Even without the leaf to help her tongue, Ganekwane finished the story. And when she had finished, the dragon said, "Another tale, Ganekwane."

When he said this, his skin burst again, and he climbed out of the old skin with a new one. And he was even smaller.

So they kept on, Ganekwane and the dragon. She told tales; he listened and asked for more. And at the end of every story, he grew smaller. When Ganekwane had told all the tales she knew, she started over again, until the dragon was so small that she could pick him up in her hand.

When the dragon saw how small he was, and how weak, he shook the way Ganekwane had shaken when he told her he was going to gobble her up. Ganekwane saw that, and she walked into the bright sunshine with the little dragon in her hand.

The people of the village watched as Ganekwane walked down the mountain, and they came out of their hiding places. They hurried towards her and said, "It's because Ganekwane is so pretty that the dragon didn't gobble her up."

"Don't forget the leaf," said her grandmother. "The leaf of the stinkwood is very strong umuthi. It helped her tongue with the tales."

Ganekwane shook her head. "No, it was the tales. Only the tales."

And Ganekwane showed them the little dragon in her hand.

When all the people stared at him, the little dragon became very bashful. His tongue shot out of his mouth, and he caught a fly.

And from that day to this, tales are told in the little village. And from that day to this, dragons fit into children's hands.